A FRIEND FOR EDDY

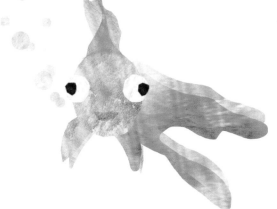

Ann Kim Ha

Greenwillow Books
An Imprint of HarperCollins Publishers

The art was created with watercolor and collaged digitally.
The text type is 20-point Argone LC Regular.

Library of Congress Cataloging-in-Publication Data

Names: Kim Ha, Ann, author, illustrator.
Title: A friend for Eddy / Ann Kim Ha.
Description: First edition. | New York : Greenwillow Books, an imprint of
HarperCollins Publishers, [2024] | Audience: Ages 4-8. | Audience: Grades K-1. |
Summary: "Eddy the goldfish makes a leap of faith to become closer
to new friends"— Provided by publisher.
Identifiers: LCCN 2023011226 | ISBN 9780063315464 (hardcover)
Subjects: CYAC: Goldfish—Fiction. | Cats—Fiction. | Friendship—Fiction. |
LCGFT: Animal fiction. | Picture books.
Classification: LCC PZ7.1.K58384 Fr 2024 | DDC [E]—dc23
LC record available at https://lccn.loc.gov/2023011226
24 25 26 27 28 RTLO 10 9 8 7 6 5 4 3 2 1
First Edition

 Greenwillow Books

For Behrang

Eddy lived all alone in his glass bowl.
Sure, he had his plants and rocks to keep him company.
But what Eddy really wanted was a friend.
Someone who could swim and blow bubbles.
Someone like him.

Eddy peered out, wondering if such a friend
would pass by . . .

One day, Eddy was playing his favorite game,
chase-your-tail, when he heard a *tap tap*.

It was a little yellow fish!

"Hi!" said Eddy. "Do you want to play with me?"
The little yellow fish nodded yes.
They played a game of tag.
Finally, Eddy didn't have to chase his own tail anymore.

The next day, Eddy heard a *tap, tap, tap, tap*.
It was the little yellow fish again,
and this time he had brought along a friend!
"Hi," said Eddy. "Do you want to play with me?"

The three of them
played hide-and-seek,

danced together,

had a staring contest,

and giggled so hard
that the bowl filled
up with bubbles.

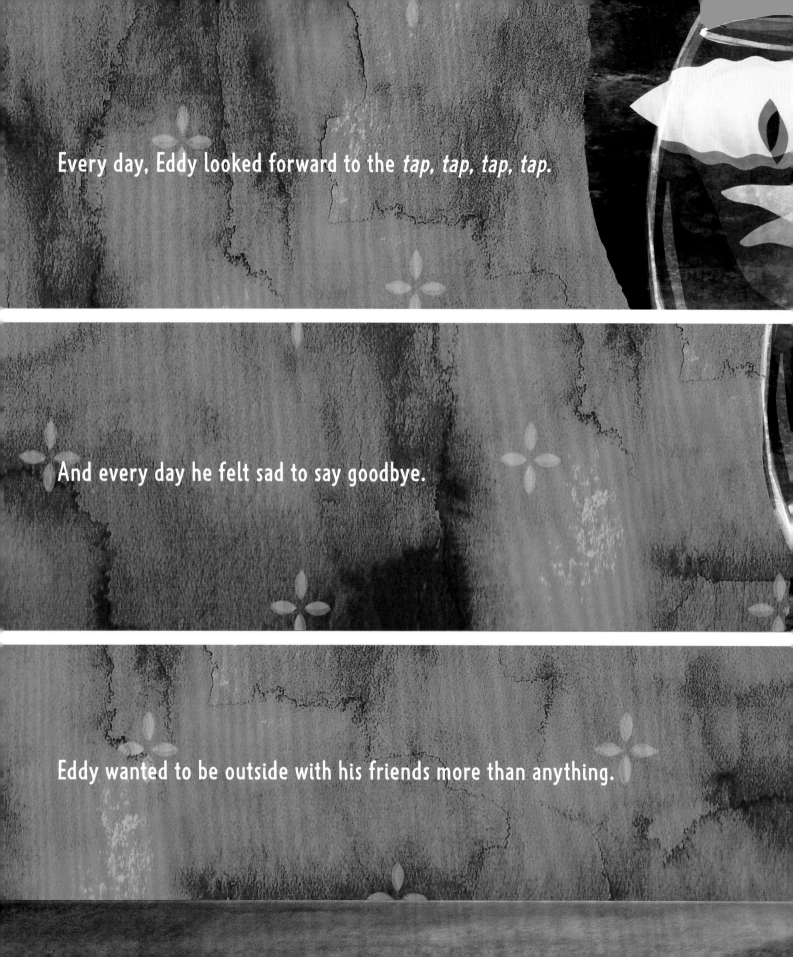

Every day, Eddy looked forward to the *tap, tap, tap, tap*.

And every day he felt sad to say goodbye.

Eddy wanted to be outside with his friends more than anything.

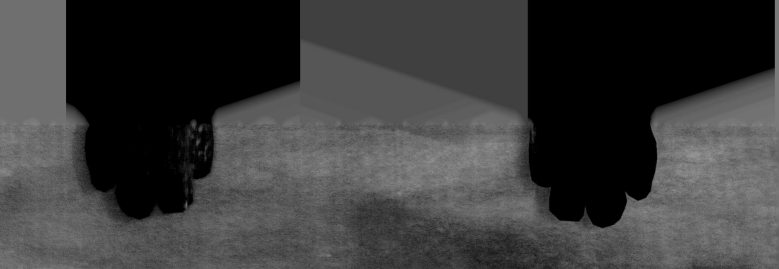

So one day, Eddy set out to do the unthinkable.
He started to swim in circles.
Slowly at first,

then faster,

and faster,

and *FASTER*,

until he launched himself out of the glass bowl!

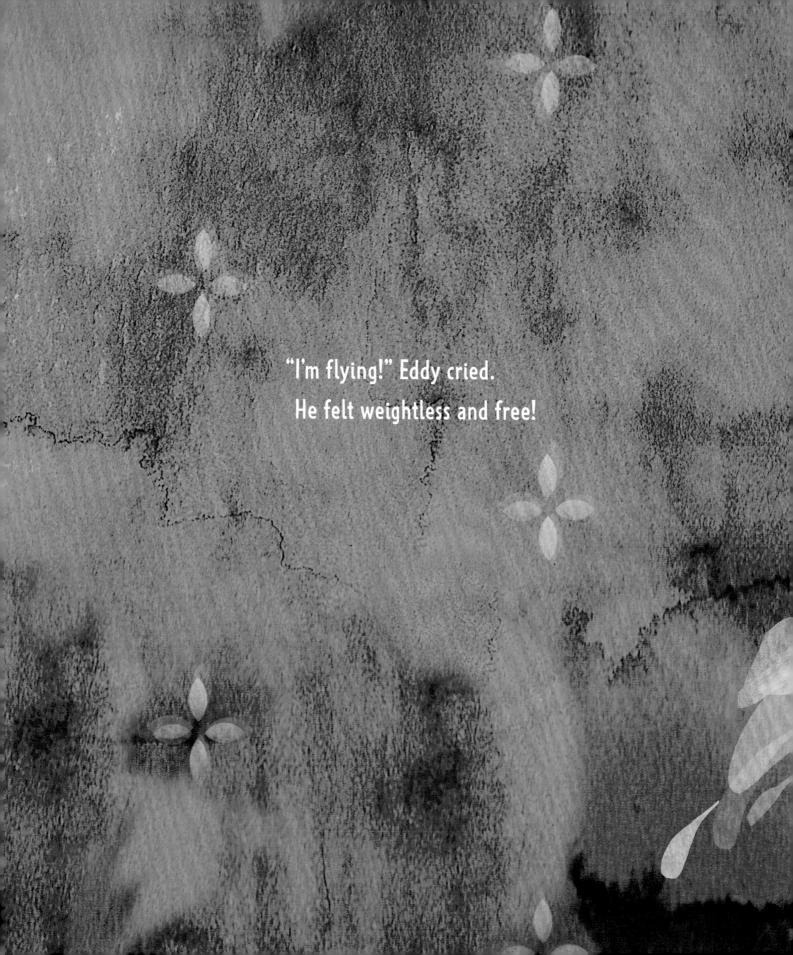

"I'm flying!" Eddy cried.
He felt weightless and free!

Eddy belly flopped hard on the table.

He couldn't swim.

He couldn't blow bubbles.

"Help!" he gasped.

Just then, the two little yellow fish appeared.
But something looked different about them.
"Those aren't my friends!" Eddy said.

Eddy flapped his tail.

He flapped harder and harder and harder.

Eddy tried to get away.

But he couldn't.

And just as he was about to give up . . .

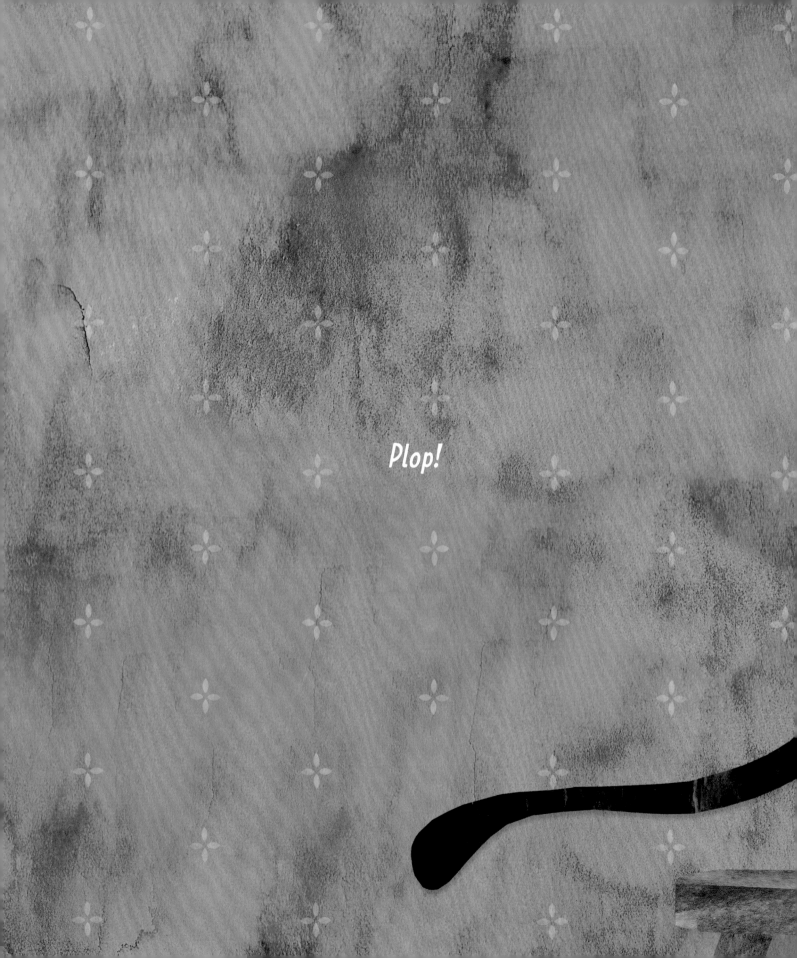

Plop!

The cool water ran through Eddy's mouth and gills.
He could finally breathe and move again.
It was a relief to be back home.

Tap, tap, tap, tap . . .

Eddy didn't see two little yellow fish this time.

He saw a cat.

A cat who had just saved him.

But most of all, Eddy saw a friend.

"I know you're not a fish," Eddy said.

"And you can't swim or blow bubbles.

But do you still want to play with me?"

"MEOW!" said the cat.

And with that, Eddy and his new friend
started a game of hide-and-seek.